Piglet Bo
is not
scared!

Written by Geert De Kockere
Illustrated by Tineke Van Hemeldonck

Translated by Thomas W. Mertens

Sky Pony Press
New York

I am never scared, thinks Piglet Bo. *Really, never. I'm not scared of anything or anyone.* Piglet Bo is sitting on a wall. He looks down. "Go away, mouse!" shouts Piglet Bo. "I am not scared of you! I'm really not!" But the mouse doesn't go away. It stays put at the bottom of the wall. "Boo!" shouts Piglet Bo. But the mouse doesn't even look up.

Piglet Bo thinks for a second. "Watch out, or I'll curl your tail!" he shouts. "And a mouse with a curled tail is really odd. Go away, mouse! Go away while you still can!"

And then, yes, right then, an angry cat appears around the corner. The mouse smells the cat coming, runs off, and disappears into a little hole.

See, thinks Piglet Bo, as he comes down from the wall, *the mouse is scared of me. I'm not scared of him. No way! I'm not scared of anything or anyone.* He looks at the hole again and quickly walks the other way.

Piglet Bo sees an open door. He walks in. It's big and dark in the room. *But I'm not scared,* thinks Bo. *I'm not scared of anything or anyone.* So he shuffles in even farther. It's really big in there. And it smells odd. "Peep?" Piglet Bo says carefully. His peep sounds hollow.

"Peep?" Piglet Bo tries again. But no one peeps back. *I've gone very far,* thinks Piglet Bo. *Maybe even twenty steps.* And he takes yet another one.

And then, yes, right then, an owl flies by. It soars right over Piglet Bo, into the dark.

Piglet Bo is startled. *Did you see that?* Piglet Bo thinks. *The owl is scared of me. But I'm not scared! I even want to go farther. But then I'll bother the owl again. That would not be nice of me. I better go back. I have to. For the sake of the owl.*

When Piglet Bo is back outside, he sees a hole in the ground a little bit farther away. A deep, narrow hole. There's a ladder sticking out. *I'll climb into the hole,* Piglet Bo thinks. *I can do it. I'm not scared of a hole.*

Piglet Bo looks over the edge. The hole looks really deep. You can't even see the bottom. "Hello!" Piglet Bo shouts into the hole. "Is anyone there?" It is silent. *I'm climbing in,* Piglet Bo thinks. *I'm not scared. I'm not scared of anything or anyone.*

But then, yes, right then, something rustles in the hole. *Hmm,* Piglet Bo thinks. *Maybe there are bugs in the hole. They might be having a party. A birthday party. And then I would be showing up uninvited.* Piglet Bo thinks some more. *No, I shouldn't do that. They would be so scared. And I didn't even bring a present. But I'm not scared. Oh no. I'm not scared of a hole.*

Piglet Bo goes around the hole and walks away. "Happy Birthday to you . . ." he sings quietly.

Piglet Bo walks past a field of nettles. He knows they sting and that will hurt. It's like your arm is on fire. *But I'm not scared of pain,* Piglet Bo thinks confidently. *So I'm not scared of stinging nettles. Oh no, I'm not. If I want, I'll jump right in. Right in the middle!*

Piglet Bo looks at the nettles. *Their sting can hurt for a long time,* Piglet Bo thinks. *Sometimes it even hurts too much to sleep. But I'm not scared. I'm not scared of anything or anyone. I'm going to jump right in!*

But then, yes, right then, a ladybug flies out of the nettle patch.
Oh, thinks Piglet Bo, *if I jump, I'll crush all the small animals in there. And then they'd be dead. Completely dead. And no one wants to die. Even if you live in the nettles.*

No, Piglet Bo thinks, *I can't jump into the nettles, no matter how much I might want to. I'm not scared, after all. Not of stinging nettles. Oh no.*

"Oh look!" Piglet Bo says. "There's a carnival!" Music is playing in the town square, and there are bright and blinking lights in every color. There's a merry-go-round and a fish pond. There's a roller coaster at the other side of the square.

Oh! Piglet Bo thinks to himself. He follows the carts with his eyes. *They go so fast! But I'm not scared of going fast,* Piglet Bo thinks. "And I'm not scared of being upside down. I'm going on the roller coaster," Piglet Bo decides.

Piglet Bo even gets a ticket. He's standing in line, waiting to get on. The little carts slow down and stop right in front of him. It's Piglet Bo's turn to get on now. "Um . . . do you maybe want to go before me?" Piglet Bo asks. "It's really no problem!" He lets everyone go in front of him, until he's the last one in line.

And then, yes, right then, the man working the roller coaster says, "It's closing time." The carts won't run anymore today. Not just for Piglet Bo. He should come back tomorrow with his ticket.

"What a shame," Piglet Bo sighs. "Because I'm not scared! Too bad I don't have time tomorrow . . ."

It's late now. Piglet Bo is getting tired. He sits against a tree. And he thinks of all the things he's not scared of. A big dog. A spider. Loud noises. A chameleon. Not even a bear. Or a lion. And he's not scared of thunder. Or lightning. Oh no. He's not scared of anything or anyone.

Piglet Bo slowly dozes off, falling deeper and deeper into sleep. When he wakes up, it's almost completely dark outside. *Oh no,* Piglet Bo thinks. *Where am I?*

And then, yes, right then, a deer makes loud and scary noises in the bushes. Piglet Bo looks around and sees large shadows everywhere. "Help! Monsters!" shouts Piglet Bo. "Don't hurt me! I taste really gross!" He jumps up and runs and runs and runs. *I'll keep running until the sun comes up again,* Piglet Bo thinks. And he's off.

No, Piglet Bo is really not scared. He's not scared of anything or anyone. Or perhaps just a bit, a tiny little bit, maybe . . .